This Little Tiger book belongs to:

_____

_____

_____

For Katinka, Leila, Bo, Raphi and
Geordie, with love ~ E-L M

For Renata, my favourite doctor! ~ L M

LITTLE TIGER
An imprint of Little Tiger Press Limited
1 Coda Studios, 189 Munster Road, London SW6 6AW
Imported into the EEA by Penguin Random House Ireland,
Morrison Chambers, 32 Nassau Street, Dublin D02 YH68
www.littletiger.co.uk

First published in Great Britain 2021
This edition published 2022

Text copyright © Emi-Lou May 2021
Illustrations copyright © Leire Martín 2021
Emi-Lou May and Leire Martín have asserted their rights
to be identified as the author and illustrator of this work
under the Copyright, Designs and Patents Act, 1988
A CIP catalogue record for this book is available from the British Library

All rights reserved • ISBN 978-1-78881-862-9
Printed in China • LTP/2700/5072/0323

4 6 8 10 9 7 5

DoctorSaurus

Emi-Lou May

Leire Martín

LITTLE TIGER

LONDON

A hundred **million** years ago
(plus three months and a day),
Some dino pals met up
to have a picnic and a **play**.

Triceratops roared, "Can't catch me!"
but didn't see the tree.
Then with a **BASH** he crashed headfirst
and broke his horn in **three**!

"There, there!" said Pterodactyl.
"I can see your horn's gone squiffy.
Let's call for Doctorsaurus
and she'll fix you in a jiffy!"

An ambulance came racing up.
It *skidded* to a stop
And out stepped Doctorsaurus
in her crisp, white doctor's top.

"Broken horns are painful,"
said the Doc, "but **no disaster**.
I'll patch it back together
with some **extra-sticky plaster**."

Then Stegosaurus sniffled,
"There's a **splinter** in my pinkie.
It's gone all **green and gooey**
and is really rather **stinky!**"

So Doctorsaurus fetched some **giant** tweezers from her kit. She pinched the pesky splinter and **removed it in one bit.**

"**Wow!**" said Doc.
"This splinter is the **biggest** that I've seen.
Your pinkie will get better now –
just keep it nice and clean."

Next snotty T-Rex plodded up.
"My nose is blocked!" he said.
"I'm **sneezing**
and I'm **sniffling**
and I've got a
thumping head."

So Doctorsaurus sat him down
and said, "Please open **wide**."
She lit her special doctor's torch
and shone the light inside.

"It's allergies!" declared the Doc.
"I bet your **eyes** feel **sore**.
But try these pills – they're perfect
for a poorly dinosaur!"

"And here's some mammoth hankies,
but there's one thing you should know –
It would be wise to warn us all
when you're about to . . .

Last of all was Brontosaurus.
"**Help!** What should I do?
My tummy's big and bloated
and I just **can't do a poo!**"

"Eat these juicy prunes," said Doc,
"they'll help unblock your tum.
You'll soon feel so much better –
and they're **really**
rather
yum!"

"Three cheers for **Doctorsaurus!**"
Pterodactyl whooped. **"HOORAY!**
Let's celebrate and scoff
our yummy picnic right away!"

The dinos munched volcano pies
and sweet Jurassic jelly.
They finished off with swamp ice cream –
so tasty but so **smelly.**

Then Doctorsaurus heard
a very rumbly, grumbly sound.
It shook the trees from top to toe
and shuddered through the ground.

"Emergency!" the Doctor cried
and waved the ice-cream scoop.
"Take cover! Brontosaurus
is about to do a . . .

"...POOP!"

The dinos gasped, "Oh, no! Look out!"
and ran away to hide,
While Bronti's stomach growled and gurgled
somewhere deep inside.

The prunes had worked and **POP!**
his tummy came unblocked at last
In one enormous **pongy, poopy,**
prehistoric blast!

"Ahhhh! That feels **MUCH** better!"
Brontosaurus grinned and sighed.
"Then let's all bop and boogie-woogie!"
Pterodactyl cried.

The dinos danced the conga
in a joyful jamboree,
And invited fifty dung beetles . . .

. . . to have the
poop
for **tea!**